Twin Flames

A collection of short stories and poems

JOHN JOE NEWBERT

Table of Contents

Preface

The following short stories and poems are dedicated to Melanie, the woman I met whilst trapped in Thailand during the COVID-19 pandemic lockdown of 2020.

Darkness

*T*he boy sat on the bus. It took an hour to return from school to his village and in all that time his face was a mask of indifference hiding the pain he felt inside.

She has left me. She has gone. She does not want me. She does not love me anymore. Thoughts swirled around and around and around inside his head. He was churning up inside as though his heart had been ripped open and all the blood was dripping in slow drops on to the floor. The pain was indescribable.

The boy's guardian angel hovered around him, invisible. She wanted to comfort him, but the boy was completely switched off. His aura was dark grey and black in places. She hovered over him trying to send him love and light, but it was impossible to break through the dark fog of pain in which he had surrounded himself.

When the bus finally stopped, he got off quickly and ran to his house. At the door, his dog greeted him, jumping up and grabbing his wrist in her mouth but the boy had no time for games today. He ran upstairs to his room and collapsed on his bed. Puzzled by his strange behaviour the dog followed him into the bedroom.

The boy began to cry. A huge sob escaped his mouth. He could not breathe. Tears rolled down the sides of his face and the dog, not understanding yet feeling his pain began to howl in sympathy.

The angel looked on. She was powerless. She put her wings around him and caressed him. She loved him. She was his spirit guide and sister soul. They had been together for eternity. She watched him cry. The boy was young to carry such pain. Why had he fallen so deeply in love? Of course, she knew why. She could see everything from her side of the veil. She understood the tapestry of life with its myriad of endless threads moving between one incarnation to another. She knew he was experiencing a karmic debt. A debt he had created for himself in another lifetime.

"I'm here," she whispered. "I'm here for you. I will always be here for you." But the boy was unable to hear her voice.

For many hours, the boy did not move. It was nighttime. He lay on his bed motionless and apathetic. The darkness enveloping his body had strengthened so the guardian angel inhaled some of it into her aura. This was her mission, to carry some of his darkness and that was also her name, Darkness.

Finally, the boy slept. His astral body exited his corporeal body and he floated beside her. She hugged the astral form which floated beside her in the air. They both looked down at the young boy's body beneath them. A thin silver cord connected the boy's astral body and the corporeal body. This connection would remain until the corporeal body breathed its last dying breath.

"It is difficult," transmitted the boy's ethereal body. "He's in a lot of pain."

"Yes," she replied. "But you will survive," she smiled. "You have to!"

The next day and the next and the next and the next all blurred into a nightmare of pain. Every day he saw the girl at school. He stopped talking to her. He thought she would miss him, but she did not. He tried to make her jealous, but it did not work. Nothing worked. And he could not understand why their relationship had come to such an abrupt and painful ending. One minute they were as happy as birds in the sky and the next it was all over.

Every night was the same. He cried himself to sleep. Darkness crept into his bed and put her angel wings around him until he fell asleep.

Whilst the boy slept the twin souls talked.

"This is not going well," he said. She agreed. She could see the miasma of darkness around the boy. There were big holes in his aura where negative entities could easily enter and cause even bigger problems for him later in life.

Summer holidays arrived and school broke up. The boy would not see the girl for six weeks. He thought of her every day. He remembered everything they had done the previous year. It seemed like a lifetime ago. As the days grew closer to returning to school, hope began to flutter in his chest again. Little stirrings of hope that she would have changed her mind. Maybe she had missed him too during the summer break. Maybe she would be happy to see him again.

Darkness watched him with sadness. She knew already what would happen.

The first day back and he took the bus to school. They shared the same syllabus and the same classes. Independently of each other, they both had made the same subject choices.

The girl no longer talked to the boy in class. Now she pretended he did not exist and as he watched her leave the classroom, he saw another boy waiting for her. They walked off hand in hand.

An icy claw of jealousy entered his heart. He was enraged. "She could not be with that imbecile," he thought. "She could not be so stupid, surely? Come on, this is not possible. What could she see in that idiot?"

The boy walked around in a daze feeling his heart slowly being shredded into tiny pieces and scattered like confetti on the floor. He felt alone in a world full of people and noise and movement. It was unreal. It could not be true. It must be a bad dream.

The angel called Darkness hovered over him trying to feed him love-light. It was impossible. The boy was unable to overcome the pain, the rejection, the jealousy, the anger, the resentment. His egoic mind tormented him ceaselessly. It seemed to delight in taking him down dark, tortuous roads which only ended in misery.

During the day, the boy managed to hide his feelings as best he could but at night, he cried himself to sleep. Finally, when he drifted off to sleep, his soul came out into the astral plane.

"This is not getting any better," he said to Darkness. "No," she agreed. "It's getting worse. Maybe I should incarnate with you in this lifetime?" she asked hesitantly.

"Yes, maybe you should," replied the boy's soul. "Because knowing myself as I do, this will go on for a long time until he learns how to heal himself."

He sighed, "Why did I agree to sign up for this?"

"Because you did," she laughed. Teasing him as she always did. "Come on," she said. "Let's go and play in the stars tonight." And off she went like a comet shooting through the night sky. He followed on her tail.

They were spinning round and round in the stars having lots of fun when suddenly Darkness stopped.

"We must ask Michael," she said.

"Ask Michael what? What are you talking about? And why have you stopped spinning?"

"I have to incarnate with you", she replied. "You're only going to have more and more problems and make more stupid mistakes and end up suffering more and I can't bear to watch that."

"I love you," he said, smiling.

"I'm serious," she said. "Let's go and talk to Archangel Michael."

"I'm already here," said Michael, his rays of azure blue shooting off in all directions into the night sky.

"I agree with you, Darkness," he said. "A new age is on the horizon and when the time is right you may incarnate."

"Not now?" Asked Darkness. "But the boy is already fifteen. I must incarnate now otherwise my human body will be too young, and the boy will be too old. I don't want to be his granddaughter...!" She laughed and laughed. The boy's soul laughed with her.

Michael smiled indulgently. Darkness had always been impatient. "I understand," he said. "Nevertheless, the boy must imagine you into existence. But I will help you. I give you my word." His blue energy faded and was gone as quickly as he had arrived.

Three years passed and the boy was still in pain. He and the girl were at a different school now and during that time he had watched the girl eat her way through several boyfriends. Every time her relationships lasted about a year yet within a few weeks she started with someone new. It was clockwork and he could not understand her.

Finally, there came a time when the boy realized he had had enough. He could not continue to cry himself to sleep for the rest of his life. Piece by piece he began to pick up the fragments of his heart and put them back together. His angel watched him with relief, happy that he had finally decided to heal. She watched him slowly arrange the metaphysical pieces into the heart shape and saw with horror the multitude of jagged scars they left behind.

Finally, the girl left school to go to university. At last, she was out of his life. But it seemed impossible that anyone else could ever live up to her image. The memory of that first time was engraved within the metaphysical scars of his heart. He had lost the ability to fall in love.

The angel held him every night in her invisible wings until he fell asleep. She was worried because his heart appeared to be dead. It worried her when she thought about what he might turn into later and she desperately wanted to join him in a physical body. She knew he would recognize her and come alive.

When the boy was twenty-one, he went to Paris, the city of love. He spent a year wandering around its magnificent streets and boulevards often thinking about love but unable to see he was preventing it from coming into his life. He had become lost and blind, and his heart was hollow. He had become a ghost of a man and no longer believed a woman could ever love him because he did not love himself.

The angel followed him everywhere. She saw everything and understood everything. She was deeply concerned. She longed to comfort him. She wanted to incarnate. She wanted to join him on the physical plane because she loved him and always had and always would. If only he was not so stubborn, she lamented.

In Paris, the young man was a teacher. One of his students became his friend and invited him round to his house from time to time, so the young man got to know his parents, especially his mother.

The mother was a small, elegant, woman in her early 40's. She had dark hair and hazel eyes. In another era, in another time, she would have been burnt at the stake as a witch. She was highly intuitive, highly spiritual and she recognized similar traits in the young man.

One warm July evening the young man had been invited to dinner. The discussion was about soul mates. Darkness was listening with interest to the conversation. She began to feel very excited. She felt that this was the moment she had been waiting for. Her young man was going to imagine her into existence.

The mother asked the young man a question – "describe your perfect woman." So, turning in his chair and looking at the empty wall he imagined a young woman standing there. She was small and slim. She had light brown skin and long, luxurious black hair. Describing her in French he finished by saying, "this is my perfect woman."

"Maybe she is only being born now," said the mother.

"Michael, Michael," cried Darkness. "It is happening. It is happening now! I can incarnate now!" She was excited. Finally, after all this time she could join him on planet earth.

The young man looked at the mother very shocked. I am twenty-two years old, he thought. How on earth can anyone imagine I could fall in love with a baby? It is ridiculous! And he forgot the incident which he considered complete nonsense.

"Michael," cried the angel.

"I know, I know, I'm looking for a vessel, but the timing is very bad. I cannot find a vessel for you. Wait, wait, I have one here. But it is not good. No, no, it is not good. It is on the other side of the world and she doesn't want the baby," said Michael.

"Darkness," he said," don't go there! There is too much pain here!"

But it was too late. She had already gone.

She

Somewhere,

Watching,

In the ether,

Regarding me here,

Smiling at my love affairs,

Feeling the beat of my heart,

As my fantasies start,

As my feelings ebb and flow,

Through my life's highs and lows,

She is always there.

She is everywhere,

In every woman I enter,

In every first hello

And every last goodbye.

She is everywhere,

Watching me,

Watching over me.

And her loving wings

Embrace me in my sleep,

In my dreams where angels weep.

The Girl Who Hated The rain

*E*verything bad seemed to happen in the rain and every time she saw the rain, she felt sad.

The first time was watching her grandfather die before her eyes. She was only seven and did not know what to do. They were at the coconut plantation and suddenly her grandfather dropped to the ground clutching his stomach. The pitter-patter of raindrops hitting the leaves and the ground echoed all around the frightened girl who did not understand what was happening.

"Grandad," she cried! Her grandfather gasped. "Girl, go and get help!" But the little girl was helpless. She was terrified and stood rooted to the spot unable to move.

The man groaned loudly. He was in agony. There was a poison eating away at his insides.

The little girl squealed in fear. She could not understand what was happening to her grandfather. The raindrops grew fatter and hit the ground harder. The man's face was covered in raindrops and his clothes got heavy and wet.

He gave one final groan and then his head hit the ground with a dull thud. The girl began to cry. Her tears mixed with the raindrops that dribbled down her face as she stood there staring uncomprehendingly at the prostrate form of her grandfather. The only sound was the constant drumming of the rain hitting the ground around her little feet.

She was twenty-three. It was her graduation ceremony. The girl was now a beautiful young woman, slim and elegant with a sweeping mane of long black hair. She was waiting for her aunty. The woman she also called mother. Alone, she watched all her friends surrounded by siblings, parents or grandparents talking excitedly amongst themselves. Outside there was heavy rain. Ominous storm clouds hovered over the university buildings and the rain suddenly came down in buckets.

The girl was feeling anxious. What had happened to her mother? Why didn't she come? She had promised to be here.

The ceremony started, and the diplomas were awarded. Everyone clapped. Everyone was happy except the young, beautiful, woman because she was alone. Her mother never arrived.

After the ceremony, she called her mum on the phone. "Sorry, I forgot," she said. The young woman walked out into the rain and her tears of desolation and resentment were washed away by a torrent of raindrops.

The woman was thirty years old. She was very beautiful, and many people looked at her as she walked quickly along the street. The men looked at her with desire. The women looked at her with envy.

It was early evening and she had just got off the plane from Singapore. It began to rain as she walked down the street towards her boyfriend's apartment. She had the key, and she was planning to surprise him. But she was nervous. She had received a tip-off from one of her friend's that he was fooling around with her cousin.

"It cannot be true, she thought. Not my cousin. Not my best friend!" But a tentacle of doubt wrapped itself around her heart.

She walked quickly, partly because of a feeling of trepidation in the pit of her stomach and partly to get out of the rain. She saw a flash of lightning and a few seconds later a crack of thunder boomed overhead.

Ducking into the doorway of the building and out of the rain she took out her keycard and slipped it into the slot of the lift and pressed sixteen. The lift shot up and deposited her on the sixteenth floor.

With a certain nervousness, she quietly made her way to the apartment. It seemed quiet and empty. Another loud crack of thunder resonated throughout the building. The rain was torrential. It was already flooding on the road outside.

She quietly opened the door and began to hear sounds from the bedroom. A man and a woman. With fear in her heart, she moved to the bedroom and flung open the door. Her boyfriend and cousin were naked on the bed. They cried out in surprise as she cried out in shock.

For a moment no one moved. Then without a word, she closed the door shut on the two of them, left the apartment slamming the door behind her and walked out onto the road.

The rain came down in sheets and soaked her to the bone, but she did not feel a thing. She only felt the immense pain of betrayal in her heart. Lightning flashed and thunder boomed overhead but she could only hear the thunder of blood pumping loudly through her body.

Everything bad happened in the rain.

Phoenix

I will shine a white light

Into the angles

Of her heart

Where her radiance

Lies dormant

In the darkroom

Of her mind.

Her radiance will arise

Scattering all shadows

unlocking her shackles

To shine in glory

In harmony with mine

The Lady Who Locked Away Her Heart

Once upon a time, there was a beautiful lady who lived alone in a castle. She had long black hair and when she stood on the top of her tower the wind caused her hair to billow out behind her like a dark cloud.

The lady lived alone. She had no desire to share her life with someone anymore. She preferred solitude. Too much sadness and grief had marked her life. So much sadness had been suffered that she had magically taken out her heart and locked it in a box in the dark dungeon of her castle so that she would never feel pain again.

One day as she stood at the top of her tower, she saw something flying on the wind far away coming fast towards her. As it got closer, she saw a man riding on the back of a dragon.

The man was a master magician who loved to travel the world on the back of his mighty blue dragon. Noticing the castle from afar he spied the lady with the long black hair. As he came closer, he saw that she was beautiful and, on a whim, decided to land his dragon and talk to her.

The dragon landed on the tower with a crunch which startled the lady. She felt angry and a little scared.

But the magician smiled and said, "Hello, don't be scared. I mean you no harm." He said it so charmingly and politely that she relaxed a little, instinctively feeling that he would not hurt her.

As they spoke the magician marvelled at this beautiful woman. Her long black hair rode on the wind behind her back. Her nose was small and refined, her mouth delicate and her eyes deep and dark. He sensed something wrong with her but could not put his finger on it. As they talked, he felt himself becoming hypnotized by her. It was as if she were casting a spell upon him, but he could not tell how she was doing it.

They talked for a long while and as they talked the magician began to see that he was falling in love with this beautiful lady. Inwardly he smiled and thought to himself it must be a subtle love spell.

Finally, he could stand it no more and said, "Lady, I believe I am in love with you".

She laughed. "Don't fall in love with me," she said. "I have no heart left. I cannot love you. You waste your time."

But the magician was very stubborn and refused to listen. He knew he was powerful and knew deep inside that the beautiful lady was his one true love. The woman of his dreams.

"Where is your heart?" He asked, perplexed by her reply.

"It's locked away in a box in my dungeon where no-one will ever reach it" she replied.

"Ha, ha, ha" she laughed. "If you can reach it you can have it," she said, knowing that it was an impossible task.

"Very well," said the magician. "Watch me! You will see."

And so saying he mounted his dragon and flew away.

The next day he returned to see the beautiful lady standing alone and forlorn on her tower.

Flying around the tower he cried a powerful spell and from the air there suddenly appeared a river of water flowing all around the castle.

"What are you doing?" cried the lady, suddenly scared by the appearance of the water.

"I'm capturing your heart," replied the magician. Without saying another word, he turned and left on the back of his powerful dragon.

The lady watched him disappear. Somehow, she felt sad and thought him a very foolish man.

For a thousand years, the lady watched the ebb and flow of the water as it rose up and down against her castle walls. Nothing happened and in time the lady forgot the magician and simply watched the ebb and flow, mesmerized by its soothing regularity.

Another thousand years passed and over time the lady began to see the effect of the water on the stone. There were flakes and chips of stone that began to crumble. She felt a tiny flicker of concern now and again.

Another thousand years passed, and the erosion of the stone walls started to look very severe. The lady was alarmed. Soon her stone walls would crack, and the water would come in. She went down to the dungeon and for the first time noticed it was damp. The water was beginning to penetrate the castle. She began to feel very alarmed and wondered what had happened to the magician.

On a bright sunny day, she spied the blue dragon in the distance coming towards her. The magician smiled when he saw her.

"You are still as beautiful as on the first day we met", he said.

"My castle! What have you done?" She cried. "You have destroyed my castle." She was very angry.

Suddenly there was a loud crack and water began to rush into the dungeon. The water picked up the box containing her heart and it floated out of the castle onto the lake.

The magician jumped on his dragon and dived down quickly to the lake where he scooped the box out of the water. Majestically he rose back to the top of the tower with the box cradled lovingly in his arms.

Dismounting he walked slowly over to the lady. She looked at him with great fear in her eyes. Her face went pale and she started to tremble.

"What are you going to do now?" she said, weakly.

"I'm going to give you back your heart and make you complete again," said the magician. And he unlocked the box with a powerful spell and the lid popped open with a squeak.

On being released for so long the heart flew out of the box straight back into the beautiful lady's chest. She fell to her knees with a groan and the magician picked her up. He lifted her up and kissed her gently on the lips.

Looking at her intently he said, "I have loved you and waited for you for three thousand years. During that time, I have travelled all over the world, but never once have I forgotten you."

The lady's heart began to beat very fast. She looked through her memories but found that the pain and sadness she had experienced in the past had all disappeared. The magician continued to look deeply into her eyes. Now it was her turn to fall under his spell.

"I have no pain anymore," she said, disbelievingly.

"I know," he replied. "I have watched you and loved you from a distance for thousands of years and the sound of the waves has cleansed and purified your heart. You are free now. All your pain has gone forever."

The beautiful lady suddenly felt a wave of gratitude and love for the magician; this man who had transformed her life. She looked at him with awe.

"Thank you. I feel so wonderful again." She hesitated and then in a soft voice, she said: "I love you too."

It was the first time in thousands of years she had spoken these words to a man.

The magician took her by the hand and helped her mount up behind him on the dragon. On its powerful wings, they shot up into the sky and flew far away, living out the rest of their lives in love and happiness and gratitude.

Starseeds

*T*he humanoid was small and blue. His skin was the colour of an evening sky with very large almond-shaped eyes of pale blue. In the middle of his forehead was a disc that shone white like crystal.

He walked into the living room of the abode he shared with his partner, Zeta. They had been together for over 700 years as counted on planet earth, but only 100 years as counted on their planet Sirius B. The humanoid was a Blue Sirian. He was an expert in deep meditation and creation. With his partner, Zeta, a singer, they could create and shape matter from the air. Shanzar, for that, was his name, was the creator and Zeta was the singer who could sing his ideas into creation. Their bonding was very deep. It was not the first time they had incarnated together and was certainly not their last.

But something was wrong. Somehow the connection had been broken. Shanzar felt deeply concerned. Normally the telepathic bond which connected them was always open. At night they frequently dreamed together as they travelled through the astral planes having fun and visiting other worlds, other places, other life forms.

Shanzar was deeply worried when he saw that Zeta had gone. He teleported to the temple of the Council of Seven – the temple where the seven wise councillors governed the planet. As if by magic the doors opened before him and he found himself standing before the Seven as if they were waiting for him to arrive.

Veldar, the eldest and most revered of the Seven spoke first:

"She has gone Shanzar, and you should wait here for her. She will eventually return. She will be reborn here again, but you must be patient."

"Why?" cried Shanzar. He felt a sharp knife of pain run through his heart. "Why has she done this? Why didn't she tell me? Why can't I go with her?"

"Shanzar, my dear friend," said Veldar, "please calm down. It is a karmic debt. Something happened a long time ago. Millions of years ago and she wanted to do this on her own. She didn't want to tell you because she knew how upset you would be for leaving you here alone."

Shanzar controlled his emotions. How could he let himself become so emotional in front of the Council of Seven? Was he an adolescent, he asked himself? He breathed deeply and released his worries and anxieties to the Holy Spirit. Immediately he became calmer.

"Veldar, what can I do? Please advise me. I need your wisdom here. How can I help her?"

Veldar paused a moment and closed his eyes. When he opened them, he looked around at the other members of the council. They had all communed telepathically. Veldar looked straight at Shanzar and said,

"Her life will be extremely difficult. She has chosen to know pain, suffering, loss, betrayal, loneliness, and abandonment. This is her mission, and it gives her tremendous potential for future growth and expansion. And a part of all that is a karmic debt. She has gone down to the prison planet on the earth plane. She is now in the third dimension."

"How can I find her and when?" demanded Shanzar. "I cannot wait here for a thousand years."

The Council of Seven held another telepathic conversation that Shanzar could not hear.

"Very well," said Veldar, "you may go down to earth but if you do this you will also suffer pain, loss, and fear. It will be very difficult for you too and you risk creating karmic debts which you will have to balance later. Are you willing to pay the price?"

"Yes", said Shanzar. "I am will willing to pay the price".

"One more thing," said the elder. "You will not meet her again until she has completed her mission. And there is a chance she will not recognize you. When we send you down to earth you will not meet her until the latter part of your human life."

"I accept," said Shanzar, delightedly. "I know I will recognize her when I see her again and I am willing to wait for her. She is my Zeta, my twin soul."

Princess Ishtar

*M*y name is Utultar, which means the divine spark of the heavenly light, and this is my story of the princess I loved and lost.

I was a powerful man in the court of King Nebuchadnezzar the second of Babylon. I had risen to become the second general in the armies of the King. I was a trusted and respected man. Many feared me for I commanded eight battalions of infantry.

Growing up close to the royal family, my grandmother had been a senior handmaiden to the Queen and for several years her advisor on Babylonian customs when the Queen first arrived in Babylon. At that time Nebuchadnezzar had been a young King and he had constructed the hanging gardens, a huge ziggurat in the centre of the city, covered in trees, bushes and flowers, to mimic the mountains and forests of Akkadia to please the Queen. I think she was happy because she bore him three children: two girls and a boy.

The boy, Prince Nergal, was one of my best friends but it was Ishtar, the youngest daughter that I fell in love with.

Nergal and I had been to the officer school for the elite military noblemen. That was where I first met him. We were the same age and we had progressed through the difficult years of military training together. Nergal had often invited me to the palace on our free days and that was where I first met Ishtar.

At first, I had not taken much notice of her: a naughty little girl running around the palace playing silly games, dressing up and hiding in cupboards. She was five years younger than I. But as the years passed and she grew up I began to notice her more and more.

I was a frequent visitor at the palace. All the palace guards saluted me every time I walked into the private quarters of the Royal family. As a close friend to Prince Nergal, I was noticed by the King who took a liking to me. Nebuchadnezzar was a very charismatic leader. I greatly respected him, and, in some ways, he became a father figure to me. Ferociously intelligent and with an iron will he was a great King. He also caused me the greatest heartache and destroyed my life.

Ishtar grew into a beautiful woman. She was small and slim. Her hair was jet black and like all the Babylonian women it was long and hung down her back like a cloak. Ishtar was smaller than her mother and elder sister. Maybe it is why I felt so protective of her. I felt she always looked up to me like an elder brother.

She had the loveliest voice I have ever heard. Sometimes she would sing for her mother and father after dinner. Those days sitting around the dinner table with the King and his family and his closest friends were some of the happiest days of my life.

One evening after dinner and perhaps too many cups of wine I wandered around the large palace gardens alone. I left Nergal inside. He was still in his cups and slightly drunk. Hearing a noise behind me I spun around and instinctively clasped the handle of my knife. It was Ishtar. She had followed me. She was seventeen and I could see the beautiful woman she was becoming.

When is the exact moment you realize you have fallen in love with someone? Perhaps it was this moment. She walked up to me and looked up at the stars.

"Do you like looking at the stars, Utultar?" She asked in a dreamy voice.

I looked at her without replying. It was the first time we had ever been alone together.

"Come." She whispered. And slipping her arm through mine she guided me into a dark, hidden area surrounded by hedges and trees. We were far away from everyone. As we lay down on the grass, side by side, she suddenly slipped her little hand into mine whilst looking up at the stars. We stayed like this for a long while. It was intoxicating. When I turned my head to look at her, I found her staring at me. Our eyes met and before I realized we were kissing each other. My arms wrapped around her shoulders and back and I held her tight in my arms.

After a few moments, she pulled away from me. She looked at me and said, "I love you, Utultar. I have always loved you."

Her words rocked me, and I realized that I loved her too. Passionately. I have never loved any woman but Ishtar. She was a Princess. My Princess. And I knew I could never have her. It cut my heart in two. Ishtar knew it also. We could never be together.

We met secretly a few more times in the garden. These were the most beautiful moments of my life. We swore our undying love and sometimes she would sing for me, quietly, under the stars, hoping that no one could hear us. She had the most beautiful voice. I will always remember her voice.

At the dinner parties when she sang romantic songs, I knew she was singing for me. She poured out her heart into those songs and although she never dared look at me in front of her father, I knew she sang for me. I was happy.

It could not last. I will never know if Nebuchadnezzar suspected something, but he called me one day for a meeting in his private audience chamber and told me he had an important mission for me. He sent me far away to Persia on a diplomatic mission. I was only twenty-two years old. One of the lower-ranking administrators and a small troop of soldiers would accompany me. It was a mission of great responsibility for one as young as I, but it meant being away for over a year.

It was impossible to see Ishtar again in private, but she sent me a medallion with a trusted servant. It was a very dangerous thing to do and perhaps she risked our lives in doing so. The medallion was gold and on the back was inscribed in tiny letters - "I will wait a thousand years for you."

I still have the medallion. It is battered and scratched from all the years and all the battles I have been through. But it is the only thing I have of her. It is my most treasured possession, and I will carry it to my grave.

When I returned to Babylon Ishtar was gone. She had been married to the king of Assyria. I never saw her again, but I cherished her for the rest of my life. I can still hear her voice in my mind. Sometimes when I hear a song she once sang for me, I weep. Even now. A lifetime later.

Perhaps…perhaps…perhaps, in a thousand years, I will meet her again, my beautiful Princess Ishtar. It is the only hope I have left.

The Parable of the Rich Man and the Poor Man

*T*here was a rich man who lived alone in a large house with many rooms. The rich man had learnt the secret of abundance. Every morning he would go out into his lovely garden and give gratitude for his abundance. He would sing to all the lovely flowers which grew around his large garden. The flowers appreciated his singing.

Over time the rich man could see that something was not quite right with his garden. Although his flowers grew well and strong, he saw that they were not as beautiful as they could be.

One day, in a flash of intuition, the rich man knew that he needed someone to sing with him in the garden. Suddenly he realized that his loneliness affected the beauty of his flowers.

Although he had abundance it was meaningless without someone to share it with.

So, he set out on a journey to find someone who would sing with him to his flowers and create perfection.

The poor man lived in a big city in a small house. His cupboards were empty, and his house was small. He spent all his time worrying and thinking about where his next meal would come from.

In his house, the poor man had one flower. It was one of the most beautiful flowers ever to exist because although the man was poor, he had been blessed with a wonderful gift. He had the power to sing into existence the most beautiful and exquisite flowers in the world. But he never had much time to use his talent. He came home tired and exhausted from work with little time to sing a song to the solitary rose which grew in a large pot beside his bed and then fall asleep.

On Sundays, the poor man would go to church and sing in the choir. His voice shone through all other voices of the congregation.

Now, one Sunday morning the rich man entered the church and heard the poor man singing. He was enraptured and he knew immediately that this was the voice he needed to sing with him in his garden.

At the end of the service, the rich man walked up to the poor man and began to talk to him.

"You have the most beautiful voice I've ever heard," said the rich man.

"Thank you," said the poor man, wondering why the rich man bothered to talk to him and what he wanted.

"I live in a faraway land," said the rich man. "I have a beautiful garden, but my flowers are not perfect, and I would like you to come and sing to them. I have a big house with many rooms," he added. "And if you want you can come and share my house and my abundance so that together, we will create the most beautiful flowers the world has ever seen!"

The poor man was taken aback. He had never seen the rich man before. He did not believe that all his problems could be solved in such a simple way. All his life he had struggled, and he could not comprehend that happiness and abundance could come so easily. He did not value his voice and therefore could not see how anyone else could put such high value on it.

The rich man continued regardless. "I know we have never met but I ask you to consider my request. I know, without any doubt in my heart, that yours is the voice I need for my flowers and my garden."

But the poor man was unable to believe the rich man and walked away. He could not believe that anyone would place such a high value on his voice. He wanted to believe but all his life struggles had taught him never to trust anyone.

The rich man walked away saddened. He knew in his heart that the poor man would have been happy. They would both have been happy, and the flowers would have been magnificent. So, the rich man went home alone to reflect on this. He wondered if one day the poor man would change his mind.

Lightness

The soul known as Lightness watched the old woman walk down the road. Her long black hair was streaked with lines of grey and her back was slightly bent. She was a little plump around the middle. Her clothes were either grey or black. A face once beautiful was heavily lined and you could see she had carried much sadness.

Lightness hovered in the air around the old woman trying to assess the amount of vital energy she carried within her body. The light was very dim and there was little life force left. She had never managed to release the burden of the suffering in her heart but now it was all coming to an end.

The woman's name was Melanie which, oddly enough, also meant darkness. The woman had experienced much darkness in her life.

Lightness had lived in a human body many, many times. He was an old soul and in his last incarnation, he had met and fallen in love with the woman, Melanie. For a very short time, they had been lovers.

Now the woman was old. Her beauty had long disappeared, and she was lonely. She still carried the memory of a long-ago, distant time when she was young and beautiful with deep regret. She remembered the immense love she had felt for the wonderful man, Lightness. But he was gone. Dead and buried in a distant land on the other side of the world.

She felt regret because she had run away. Too afraid of being hurt by his promises and dreams of happiness she ran away from him. What a fool she had been. She felt so alone and sometimes, even after all the years in-between she still felt little twinges of pain inside her heart.

Today she felt more than a twinge of pain. She put her hand to her heart. It gave a strange spasm and then she felt a flaring of pain erupt in her chest. Her body fell to the ground. It became inert. Life suddenly extinguished.

Slowly the soul that was Darkness exited the body. Her light was so much, much, brighter outside of the body. She was a globe of shimmering silver light of exquisite beauty. She was radiant. Incandescent.

Lightness hovered closely watching his twin leave the body of the woman, Melanie.

"Why did you leave him in this lifetime.?" He asked. "They would have been so happy together!"

"I know," she sighed. "But she let her ego get in the way. She was confused and afraid. I am sorry Lightness. I could not do anything. I tried but she would not listen to me. She blocked me out and switched me off".

"But now I am free again!" She laughed with joy.

The two souls coalesced into One and disappeared into another dimension.

Printed in Great Britain
by Amazon